Blizzard-Boy

Book I: A New Hero

Robert Keller

Chapter 1

"The Superhero Training Academy of Thanta, or STAT, is home to some of the greatest superheroes in the world. The academy was designed as a way for supers to have formal training that would allow them to be able to be more prepared whenever danger strikes. Although there are several other academies, STAT is the most well-known of them due to its immense size and centralization in the region of Thanta. The other academies answer to STAT as it is considered the control center to them. It is in relation to this that I believe that STAT is an important part of our history."

"Superheroes have long been thought to simply be like in the comics where they fight the bad guys and save the day. However, history at STAT has shown otherwise as the reality of the situations around us do not always lead to victory. This is what has resulted in STAT's motto: 'Success is not measured in the number of villains defeated but rather in lives saved.' The superheroes at STAT work diligently to protect those without powers and prevent the world from being taken over by supervillains. Their actions are the reason that Thanta has thrived and grown into a safe place. That concludes my report."

"Thank you, Robert, for a wonderful report," the teacher said. "You may be seated."

I walked back to my desk and sat down. I couldn't gauge how the class reacted even though many of my friends loved superheroes. The rest of the reports consisted of other businesses around the city that had a direct influence. My decision to write on the Superhero Training Academy of Thanta was based solely on my love for heroism. I sat and listened to the other reports, but not without daydreaming about what it would be like to be a superhero. As the final report finished, I looked up at the clock. 2:59. One more minute and I would be released from school.

"Thank you everyone for the wonderful reports," the teacher said to us. "There were many unique businesses and reports, but the rubric I passed out to you will be what I use to grade each one of your papers. Remember to do your homework tonight on chapter seven and be prepared to talk about it tomorrow in class."

The bell rang and everyone sprung out of their seats. I gathered my things and began walking toward the door. Before I could get out, I heard my teacher call out for me. I turned around and walked over to her.

"You called me?" I asked her.

My teacher looked up at me. "Yes, I did," she said. "I wanted to have a chat with you about your report."

My heart began to sink. "What's wrong with it?" I asked.

"Your report was very interesting and enticing, but I'm not quite sure I understand how it fits into the overall prompt," she said. "I know how much you love superheroes, but STAT is not really considered a business under the criteria. It is not really a place that someone can go to and request to be hired."

I nodded my head. "I tend to think of businesses in a different way," I said. "When I think of a business, I think of anything that can provide a service to the greater population. For me, that service that STAT provides is protection from the villains and evil around us. It's not a normal service, but I always find it to be fascinating."

"Regardless, there were specific guidelines that I asked you to follow when choosing a business and this went against those guidelines," she said to me. "Although your prompt is well written and I understand your point, I do have to follow the rubric and I will have to take away points from your overall paper."

I hung my head. "I understand," I said.

My teacher smiled. "It won't be many points though, but I suggest you pay more attention to the prompts next time," she said. "Now run along and head home. I don't want you to miss out on the beautiful weather this weekend."

I nodded and headed out the door. I made my way down the hallway and looked at all the other students. Many were staying for afterschool activities or to meet with friends. I never really fell into those categories because I

7

preferred to study more about the superheroes in Thanta. I made my way out of the school and instantly felt the warmth of the sun hit my shoulders. Summer was only a few weeks away, but it felt so much closer.

Being only 14, I never put myself in any kind of dangerous or risky situation. I had always wondered what it would be like to be a superhero or to even do a job that was like that. My whole purpose for studying the things I did was to prepare myself for the real world. I looked down the street and began my walk back to my house. The walk home is always peaceful. The town of Motrac has never been a hustle and bustle town; rather, it is a slower paced town. Walking or riding a bike is a commonality in Motrac and the people are very friendly. My house resides on the outskirts of town, requiring me to cross the bridge over the Thanta river. It is a very scenic route with a lot to look at.

As I began my walk home, I could hear children playing on the playgrounds. Their laughter could be heard from miles away as I could hear them playing tag and hide-and-seek. The wind was slight and swayed the branches of the trees ever so slightly. It was a crisp, clear day and I was ready to get home and enjoy the sunshine. Step by step, I hummed some tunes to help me get home faster.

I made my way around the corner and saw the bridge in the distance. I knew I wasn't too far away now, and I was moving much more quickly. Moving at a brisk pace, I passed by many kiosks around the streets and listened to the sounds of people buying and selling their products. I wasn't paying attention and slammed right into someone. I hit the ground hard and heard them do the same. I immediately got up and walked over to them.

"I'm so sorry! I wasn't paying attention to where I was going," I said to the person.

They looked up at me and I instantly recognized the person. She had dirty blonde hair and bright blue eyes. "It's alright," she said to me.

"You're… you're… you're Aqua-Gal?!?!" I stammered. "From STAT?"

She nodded her head. "I train there every day, but today is my day off of training so I am taking in the sights and sounds," she said.

My face lit up knowing I was talking to an actual superhero. "What's it like there?" I asked her.

"It's such a nice place to train," she said. "There are so many supers and there is so much to do. There are hundreds—if not thousands—of different training arenas set up to suit each element or power. The classes are so helpful and everyone is friendly."

"Wow that's amazing!" I said. "I wish I were a superhero."

Aqua-Gal looked away. "It has its perks, but there are times that I wonder what it would be like to live a normal life," she said. "That's why I often come out to the towns around STAT to see what it's like to not have to defend the world day after day."

I nodded in agreement. I had never thought about how stressful and time consuming it could be to be a superhero. Leading a normal life would seem difficult since everyday would be spent training or preparing for missions. It didn't matter to me though because I wanted to live that kind of life anyway. My family would never be accepting of that lifestyle, but it didn't matter to me.

"Well, it was nice to meet you... what did you say your name was?" Aqua-Gal asked me.

"I'm sorry I never introduced myself," I said. "My name is Robert."

"Nice to meet you Robert," she said. "I have to get going because I'm meeting up with some other supers for a night on the town."

"I won't hold you up then, but if you're ever looking to have a moment of normalcy away from the superhero life I can always be of assistance," I offered.

Aqua-Gal smiled. "I'd appreciate that," she said. "Thanks again and I'll catch you later!"

"Later!" I said to her. I watched as she walked back into the town. I couldn't believe I actually met a real superhero! I turned back toward the bridge and began heading home. I got to the bridge and carefully made by way across. The bridge had been wearing down for a while, but it was in the process of being fixed. To the east of the bridge was an old chemical plant. The plant had been used for experimental chemicals, but it was never announced or released as to what these chemicals were supposed to be. It had been abandoned about 5 years prior due to lack of funding, but there had always been speculation that some of the experiments had been illegal.

I finished crossing the bridge and turned the corner to reach my house. I lived out in the outskirts away from the main city life because my parents did not want to be caught up in all the drama within the town. Farmland spanned all around the houses and I loved the view of the country. I got to the front door and grabbed the doorknob. As I turned the knob, I noticed the note on the mailbox from my mom. It read:

Robert, we have gone into town to get groceries and other things we need for the week. Make sure you have your homework done by the time we get home at 5. Love, mom.

I smiled knowing that any time my parents go into town for groceries, it usually means that we are having a big meal. I opened the door and set my backpack down on the ground. I dug out my notebook and textbooks and went to my room to start my homework. I set my stuff on the desk and opened everything up. Next to my desk was my music player so I hooked it up and put the headphones in my ears. I then began to work on my homework.

As the time passed, I had finished my homework and was now doing more research on superheroes. I had about a half hour before my parents would be home and I wanted to use the time to do more research. I got engrossed in a book called *50-year legend* that I had failed to watch the clock. The book had read:

Legends of a so-called 50-year super have been recorded during the battle of darkness. As Thanta became shrouded in darkness, it was said that the 50-year super brought forth the beam of light that restored order and peace to the land. However, the super was never seen nor heard from after the battle, leaving some to speculate whether the events that occurred were factual or simply a passing of eclipses.

I finally looked up at the clock and saw that it said 7:30 PM. I quickly closed the book and went downstairs, worried that my parents had called me several times for dinner. However, there was no smell of cooked food nor the sound of my parents rustling in the kitchen. I looked around the house calling out for them but got no answer. It was unusual for my parents to be this late getting home, but not unheard of. There have been a few times where they have gotten caught up meeting up with people they knew and simply lost track of time. I went back to my room and pulled out my phone to call them. I got their voicemail both times. I called my mom one last time and left a voicemail.

"Hey mom it's me," I started. "I was just wondering where you guys were at. I know your note said 5 but I figured maybe you guys got caught up in other business. Just give me a call and let me know what's going on. I love you."

I hung up and went back to reading my book. I kept reading and I could feel my eyes getting heavy. The next thing I knew, I was awoken to the sound of pounding on the front door. I jolted out of bed and looked at the clock. 9:45 PM. I rushed down to the door thinking that they couldn't open the door with their hands full. I opened the door and saw a police officer standing at the door.

"Are you by chance Robert?" The officer asked me.

I nodded my head. "Yes sir," I said. "What's this about?"

"May I come in?" He asked me.

"Yeah sure," I said. "My parents aren't around at the moment though if that's who you're looking to talk to."

The officer shook his head. "I need to speak with you. It's about your parents," he said.

My heart began beating faster. "What about them?" I asked cautiously.

"Let's have a seat," he said.

I nodded and guided us to the living room. I turned on some lamps along the way as we sat down in the living room. At this point, the only thing that my head could register was the sound of the grandfather clock ticking behind me. The officer looked at me and took a deep breath.

"My name is officer Bradford," he said. "I apologize for coming at this time of night, but this is important. Your parents were out in town today shopping, correct?"

I nodded my head. "My mom left me a note saying they would be back around 5, but they still haven't come home."

Officer Bradford looked down and I felt my heart sink. "What happened to them?" I questioned.

"Your parents were on their way home when they were struck by a car that ramped up the curb. They were severely hurt and rushed to the hospital, but unfortunately passed away about an hour ago," he said to me.

I just stared at him. I didn't know what to say. I was trying to fight back tears, emotions, anything that would cause me to overreact. The pain was coursing through my body, and I felt as though the world had punched me in the gut multiple times and left me laying on the ground. I didn't want to believe it; I couldn't bring myself to believe it. Tears were filling my eyes.

"I don't… how did…" I couldn't find the words. The reality was sinking in too hard and too fast for me. I didn't want to be here. I couldn't hold

14

onto the pain. I did the only thing my brain could think to do: run. I got up and ran out of the house, officer Bradford calling me with every step I took. The tears were streaming down my face. Every step grew heavier than the last. My parents couldn't be dead. I knew if I rushed into town, I would find them talking to friends, family, even shop owners. They weren't gone, I knew they weren't. I rushed across the bridge and into town. I started calling for them. My calls quickly turned into yells, then screams, and finally weeping. I fell to my knees and cried. No matter what I wanted to believe, the truth was in front of me: my parents were dead. I pounded my fists into the ground and screamed.

"What's going on? What's wrong?" I heard someone asked from behind me. I instantly recognized it. I turned around and saw Aqua-Gal standing behind me.

"Aqua-Gal," I said between tears. "What are you doing here?"

"I was patrolling the town to make sure that everything was calm, and I heard you scream. What happened?" she asked genuinely concerned.

I hung my head and said, "Aqua-Gal... my parents are dead."

She stood there and extended her arms out. I threw myself into her embrace and cried. She didn't say a word to me; she let my emotions flood out. I cried until it hurt to cry and then I felt numb. Everything in my body was weak and tired. I lost all the energy I had and wanted to sleep. Aqua-Gal looked at me and nodded.

15

"Let's get you back to your house," she said. "I'll stay there and watch over the house until the morning. Then I'll help get things settled as to what needs to be done for you."

I nodded mustering all the strength I could. Aqua-Gal walked beside me as we headed back toward my house. We were silent as my head was still trying to wrap itself around the whole situation. We reached the bridge and began to cross. As we got halfway across, we both felt a small rumble and stopped.

"What was that?" I asked.

"I'm not sure," Aqua-Gal said. "Whatever it was— "

Her words were cut off by the sound of an explosion. We fell over and saw the explosion had come from the chemical plant. Shrapnel was flying in every direction with some of it heading our way. Aqua-Gal got up and began to launch aqua jets at the pieces of shrapnel to knock them away. Piece after piece went flying and Aqua-Gal defended the two of us. Just then, a large piece about the size of a large rock came sailing past and was headed right toward me. I rolled to get out of the way, but I didn't move fast enough, and the sheet metal sliced part of my arm. I screamed in pain as a burning sensation filled the wound and I knew something wasn't right. Aqua-Gal turned around and gasped.

"We have to get you out of here!" she said.

Just then, another explosion occurred, and more shrapnel started falling. Aqua-Gal pointed to the other side of the bridge and I nodded. I got up and stumbled my way across the rest of the bridge, dodging piece after piece. As I was about to finish crossing, more sheet metal fell and struck my leg leaving another open wound. The burning sensation intensified and I cried out in pain. I made it to the other side and fell to the ground. Everything around me was starting to get fuzzy and dark. I tried calling out to Aqua-Gal who was still fighting off shrapnel as she worked her way back over, but I never figured out if she made it unscathed. The pain and whatever else was coursing through my body got the best of me and I blacked out.

Chapter 2

I could hear voices talking and hear things moving. It wasn't audible enough for me to be able to understand what they were saying, but whatever it was had to do with me. I wanted to open my eyes, but my body wouldn't will them open. I waited and listened carefully, but I could only make out a few words.

"Bridge... explosions... a lot of damage... chemical... should have been dead," Was all I could make out. I figured it meant that whatever had happened should have killed me. I must've fallen into a coma or been induced into one because I couldn't remember a thing. A few more minutes passed and I finally started opening my eyes. I saw the people turn at look at me. I could make out a group of doctors.

"He's waking up," one of them said.

Another doctor walked up to me. "You're lucky to be alive son," he said. "That shrapnel and the chemicals on it should have killed you rather quickly."

My vision slowly cleared more and I carefully nodded my head. I began to feel slight twinges of pain in my arm and leg, and I remembered the cuts. I looked at them and saw gauze patches wrapped around them. The doctors recognized where I was looking and addressed them.

"You suffered some seriously deep cuts on your arm and leg. The cuts didn't go deep enough to the veins, but they were awfully close to severing them. We had to stitch them up to prevent blood loss. Unfortunately, we were unable to clean out all the chemicals out of the system, so we have been trying to flush it out through the IV fluids. It appears to be working since you are alert, but we won't know for sure until the latest blood tests come back. Until then, you'll need to stay here for examination," the doctor informed me.

I sat up slightly and looked at them. "Aqua-Gal?" I carefully said.

"She's safe," the first doctor said. "She's actually outside waiting to see you. Would you like for her to come in?"

I nodded and the doctors walked out. I looked around the room and noticed a lot of different things. The tools and medicines were different from ones that I remembered. I also noticed some of the books on the shelves were different. I couldn't make out the titles, but my focus was broken by the sound of the door opening. I saw Aqua-Gal walk in and I smiled.

"I'm glad to see you're awake," she said. "I was afraid you had died."

"What happened?" I asked her, struggling to get words out.

Aqua-Gal sat in a chair next to the bed. "You got hit by some of the sheet metal and it cut you up pretty well," she said. "The cuts themselves

19

weren't what caused you to black out though. It was the chemical components on them that caused a negative reaction."

"What chemicals were they?" I asked.

"Some of the chemicals were just standard things, but there was one in particular that was more potent than the rest," she said. "This chemical was classified to the rest of the world due to the nature of it, but since you wound up having some inside your system, it's only fair that you know about it."

"When the chemical plant was in operation, there were a lot of experimental chemicals being worked on. I'm sure you know that much since it was all over the news. There were some chemicals that were being created to try to help with cleaning or even corrosion, but there was one that caused the plant to get shut down. They were working on a type of perpetual chemical that wouldn't require changes to release energy. It was supposed to be a universal chemical called Zalcia."

"This chemical was being experimented without the government's knowledge because of the types of chemicals being used. It was almost considered a failed chemical until they got the reaction they were looking for about 5 years ago. The energy being released from it was ten times more power than a standard electrical grid. It created so much energy that it nearly caused a chain explosion in the plant. Government officials found out about this and immediately shut down and quarantined the plant. Unfortunately, this experimental chemical had not been studied enough to understand its full properties, so there was no knowing the half-life of it. The government had been working to regulate the chemical plant to have it destroyed, but the uncertainties surrounding it were too great. Thus, the plant was simply left abandoned with no knowledge as to why for the rest of the world."

I nodded. "How did you find out about it?" I asked.

"Superheroes were told by the government because we have an upper hand in the protection area if something would happen. No one foresaw the explosion the other night at the plant, but right now it looks like just a meltdown until we finish investigating," she said.

"What do you mean the other night?" I asked. "How long have I been out?"

"Almost three days," she said to me.

My eyes grew wide. "What about school and my family?" I asked, struggling to say family.

"They know you're safe and we explained the situation as best as we could," she said. "Right now, you need to be here where you can get healed up properly."

I looked around. "Where exactly is 'here'?" I asked.

Aqua-Gal smiled. "You're in the hospital area of the Superhero Training Academy of Thanta," she said.

I grew excited knowing that I was in STAT. "Are you serious?" I said. "This has been my life dream! Well... maybe not in this fashion."

Aqua-Gal chuckled. "I figured you would be excited," she said. "We have the best medical care team here that will monitor and take care of you."

I nodded suddenly feeling slightly weak again. "I think I need to rest some more," I said.

Aqua-Gal nodded. "I'll let you rest, and the doctors will check up on you occasionally to make sure you are doing alright," she said.

She got up and started walking to the door. "Aqua-Gal," I called to her. She turned around and looked at me. "Thank you... for everything." I said to her.

Aqua-Gal smiled. "You don't need to thank me," she said.

Aqua-Gal walked out the door and carefully closed it. I laid my head back down and began to doze off. I found myself back in my house with the lights turned down. I looked around and everything seemed normal. I could smell food cooking and hear my parents talking and laughing. I walked into the kitchen to see them cooking and having a good time. They turned around and saw me and smiled. They motioned toward the table and I sat down. They brought food over and we ate and talked. As we finished, they got up and cleared the dishes. Just then, a car crashed through the side of the house right into where my parents were standing. I called out to them, but it was already too late. In that instant, my parents disappeared in thin air. My body grew cold and weak again and I could see the world melting around me. I screamed out and cried out to them, but everything was disappearing. I ran and yelled but it was doing no good. My body grew numb and I felt the cold surround me more.

"Wake up Robert!" I heard someone call to me.

I jolted myself awake and realized I was dreaming. However, I still felt cold in the body and numb and I didn't understand why.

"Get up out of the bed!" I heard a doctor say to me. I looked over at him and nodded.

As I got up, I turned around and gasped. My entire bed was a complete sheet of ice. My body imprint was all around it and I couldn't figure out what happened.

"Are you ok?" the doctor asked me.

"Yeah," I said. "Where did all of this ice come from?"

The doctor looked at me. "This is going to sound crazy, but it came from you," he said.

I gave him a puzzled look. "I don't understand," I said. "How could this have come from me?"

The doctor shrugged his shoulders. "I was in here checking your vitals when I saw ice pouring onto your bed," he said. "It appeared to be coming out of your hands, but I couldn't be certain."

23

I grew more confused. "I don't have superpowers though," I said. "I couldn't have created the ice."

Just then, I felt something leaking out of my hand and I looked to see ice slowly coming out of my hand. I screamed and fell back in shock. I didn't know what was going on, but it was starting to freak me out. I couldn't figure out if I was still dreaming or if this was really happening. The ice slowed down and stopped, and I didn't know what to do.

"What's going on??" I demanded.

"It appears as though you somehow gained superpowers," the doctor said.

"That's impossible!" I said. "Superpowers can't be gained or learned. It's only found in genetic coding, and I clearly didn't have that."

The doctor walked up to me and helped me up. "I'm just as confused as you are, but there may be a reason behind it." He said. "Although we are still trying to fully understand the situation, it appears that the Zalcia in your system may have contributed to the gaining of superpowers."

I shook my head. "This can't be real," I said. "Some random chemicals can't just give me superpowers. This isn't a comic book!"

"You have to understand that we don't fully understand the properties of Zalcia, so this is all speculation. Your blood still shows a high concentration of Zalcia content which has led us to believe that maybe the chemical has more

24

properties than we realize. This might have been why the superheroes were alerted of the creation of Zalcia, but we will never know since the only area that Zalcia has existed is now gone," the doctor said to me.

I shook my head in disbelief. "This is all so much happening at once," I said. "Everything is happening and I don't understand why."

The doctor nodded as the door opened and Aqua-Gal walked into the room. She looked at the bed of ice and gasped. "What happened??" she asked confused.

"Apparently, I did it," I said. "I don't even know what is happening."

"Aqua-Gal, can I speak to you outside really quick?" the doctor asked her.

Aqua-Gal nodded and the two of them stepped outside the room. I took time to take in what was going on. I got my phone off the table and did a search about Zalcia. Just like they had said, there was no information about it in existence. Whatever this chemical was, it was causing a change inside me that I didn't understand. Somehow, it was giving me superpowers and I just had to accept that this was going to be the case. Just then, Aqua-Gal came back into the room.

"Robert," she said, "It looks like you probably do have superpowers. I don't know how to explain it or even why it's happening, but whatever the case maybe you now have superpowers."

I nodded. "I guess I just have to accept it until we understand exactly what is happening," I said.

"The doctors are going to come back and take a DNA sample and do some analysis on it to see what they can come up with," she said. "We are all in agreement that there is a possibility that the Zalcia may have either altered or added DNA in your body to give you superpowers."

"So, what happens to me then?" I asked. "Do I just go home and live with this ice?"

Aqua-Gal shook her head. "You have a superpower that is uncontrolled which means you need training," she said. "Your life dream is about to come true. Welcome to the Superhero Training Academy of Thanta!"

Chapter 3

"When you meet the Superleader, that's where you'll have to pick out your superhero name," Aqua-Gal said to me as we walked out of the hospital.

"I already have one figured out," I said.

"Oh yeah? What is it?" she asked.

I smirked. "You'll have to wait until we get there," I said.

Aqua-Gal smiled. "I know this is a lot to take in, but STAT will take good care of you," she said. You'll be able to live in your house since three other supers live in that area as well."

"Who else lives near me?" I asked confused. "I've lived there for years and never noticed any other supers."

Aqua-Gal laughed. "Or so you thought," she said.

I gave her a quizzical look as we approached the front doors of STAT. The building itself is massive to begin with, but the size of the front doors makes it seem even larger. It had to reach at least 11 feet high and span at least 6 feet for each door. The hiss of the automatic doors opening made me feel giddy knowing I was about to enter the superhero world. Once I stepped inside, I was not disappointed.

The lobby itself was massive. Tall pillars line the sides of the lobby with plants set up next to them. In the center of the lobby was the reception desk where superheroes would check in and out of the building. Beautiful paintings of the different regions in Thanta were along the walls along with photos of some of the other training academies. I recognized the Superhero Training Academy of Mountain Pontic from when I was a kid, but the others were new to me. We walked up to the reception desk and were greeted by the receptionist.

"Hi Aqua-Gal!" she said cheerfully.

"Hey Sammy," she said. "We're here to see the Superleader. This is Robert."

I waved to her. "Hi," I said.

She smiled at me. "Hi Robert! Nice to meet you!" she said. "The Superleader is just finishing up in a meeting so if you want to wait outside his office, he should be there shortly."

"Thanks again Sammy," Aqua-Gal said.

We began walking through the rest of the lobby. "Is Sammy a superhero?" I asked Aqua-Gal.

Aqua-Gal shook her head. "She is one of two people in STAT who are not superheroes," she said. "The other is Tommy who works as the training room coordinator. It's part of an effort to try to create a hybrid atmosphere between supers and normal people. We only have those two positions because

28

they do not require any combat action. It allows more superheroes to be readily available should a mission arise."

I nodded and continued to take in the sights and sounds. Superheroes were lining the length of the hallways chatting and laughing. Some were even showing off their powers to others. We turned one more corner and found ourselves looking down toward the Superleader office. I had only read a few things about the Superleader position, so I didn't know what to expect. I was excited and nervous at the same time.

"Don't worry," Aqua-Gal said, apparently sensing my nervousness. "The Superleader is very friendly and is excited to meet you."

"I'm just nervous because I'm not like the other supers," I said. "They were born and raised with their powers, and I gained mine in a strange way. I don't even have control of my powers!"

"There are plenty of superheroes here who don't have control of their powers," she said. "There's even an entire class dedicated to it. Just because superheroes are born with powers doesn't mean they know how to control it."

I sighed and looked down. I knew she was right, but it was hard to fathom the number of changes I was about to go through to adapt to this new lifestyle. I then heard footsteps and I looked up to see someone coming down the hallway. The person was tall—maybe 6 feet or so—and was fairly muscular.

He had short brown hair and deep brown eyes. He stepped up to us and held out his hand.

"I presume you are Robert, correct?" He asked.

I took his hand and shook it. "Yes sir," I said.

He smiled and said, "I am the Superleader of the Superhero Training Academy of Thanta. My formal name is Fraxion, but you may call me the Superleader if you wish."

I nodded. "Nice to meet you," I said nervously.

Fraxion laughed. His laugh was booming. "No need to be nervous son!" he said. "I know this is all new to you and that's why I'm here. Please, step into my office."

He opened the door and Aqua-Gal and I stepped into his office. It was very spacious with a lot of bookcases around the room. His desk sat in the middle with a nice chair behind it. Stacks of paper lined the top of the desk in neat piles. It appears they were organized well, and the room was very tidy. I sat down in a chair across from the desk and Aqua-Gal did the same. Fraxion walked over to one of the bookcases and grabbed a book. He opened it and flipped through the pages.

"Do you know the story of the superhero in Groundlock?" Fraxion asked me.

"No sir I don't think so," I said politely.

Fraxion looked over to me. "His name was Blazit. He was the most renowned superhero to come from the region of Groundlock. I assume you know where Groundlock is located?"

"I have a general idea," I said. "Isn't it near the forest on the other side of Motrac?"

Fraxion nodded. "Blazit was a superhero like you. He gained his powers at a later age than most and struggled to control his powers. He was one of the more challenging students because he had an attitude like fire. In the end, he became one of our most brilliant students and even went on to become an elder in the region of Groundlock."

"An elder?" I asked confused.

Aqua-Gal turned to me. "Elders are designated to each region to oversee the shrines of the elements to ensure that villains and regular people do not trespass on its grounds," she informed me. "Each region is comprised of an elemental attribute and thus has a shrine of the element that possesses that power. For the region of Thanta, it houses the water element."

"Very good Aqua-Gal," Fraxion said. He then turned back to me. "The point of this story is that it will seem like an uphill battle to control and harness your powers, but as long as you stay with the course and follow your training, you will do just fine."

I nodded. "I just don't understand how I got the superpowers in the first place," I said. "I didn't even have any genetic background related to superheroes."

Fraxion walked back to his desk and sat down. "To be honest, I'm not even sure how it is possible," He said. "You are incredibly unique in that regard, but nevertheless, you now possess the powers of a superhero and as such must learn the ways of the super. We will all work together to research and discover the truth behind this phenomenon, but until then you will begin with regular training."

He handed me the book he was holding. I took it and read the title. *Superhero Training Academy of Thanta Official Handbook.* I never thought I would have held this book in my hands, but the circumstances had changed and now I was about to dive into the superhero realm.

"Keep this book and use it as a guideline," Fraxion said. "It is less of a rules and regulations book and more of an advice and guideline book. It will give you suggestions when you are unsure of how to proceed. Study it and hold it with care as it contains many secrets and details about our academy."

"Yes sir," I said. "I won't lose it."

"Good," Fraxion said. He then dug through some papers and pulled out a couple forms. "Since you are now becoming a part of the STAT family, you will have to decide on a superhero name. There are plenty to choose from and I even have a list that— "

"Blizzard-Boy," I said.

Fraxion nodded. "It seems like you've already thought this out," he said.

"I was the kid in school who wanted to learn more about superheroes, even become one," I said. "I did research, drew pictures, even imagined what it would be like. I've had this name for the longest time, and it seems like it fits pretty well considering my power."

As I was speaking, I noticed my chair felt cold and I snuck a glance down and saw that the bottom of the chair had frozen. I tried to hide my embarrassment, but Fraxion simply laughed.

"There's no shame," he said. "This is all part of the training to become a superhero!"

I nodded and tried to break the ice. Fraxion started writing on the forms and then handed them to me to sign.

"These forms state that you are officially becoming a part of STAT and that your new official name will be 'Blizzard-Boy' from now on," Fraxion said. "This includes when you talk to people on the streets. The reasoning for this is to protect your family and friends who might not be superheroes."

I hung my head. "I don't have a lot of family to protect anymore," I said. "My parents were killed a few days ago by a car."

Fraxion got serious. "I'm sorry to hear that son," he said. "I know it can be tough, but channel that pain away from yourself and use your heart to fight for the right cause. We've had a number of superheroes who have allowed these kinds of tragedies to consume them, and it has destroyed them in the end."

I nodded. "I will do my best sir," I said.

"That's what I want to hear," Fraxion said.

I looked down at the papers and read them over. These were the official documents that would change me from a normal human to a superhero. I took a deep breath and grabbed the pen. I began to sign my name on the lines and handed the forms back to Fraxion. He looked them over, then held out his hand.

"Congratulations on becoming a member of the Superhero Training Academy of Thanta, Blizzard-Boy!" he said.

I reached out and shook his hand. "Thank you, sir," I said.

"You are only slated for one program right now," Fraxion said. "That is to help you control your powers. You are welcome to the training rooms from B13 through B45. These are specially designed with a meditative section to allow you to work on your control. All other training rooms you must be accompanied by another super until you have passed the program. This program runs from 9AM to 1PM each day. Do not be late to it!"

"Understood," I said.

Fraxion smiled. "Go ahead with Aqua-Gal and check out the rest of the facility," he said. "We'll be waiting for you in your program tomorrow morning!"

Aqua-Gal and I got up and stepped out of the office. We closed the door and I exhaled. This would be the start of my new journey. I was about to begin my superhero training and leave my old life behind. The excitement started coming back and that's when I knew I was ready.

Robert was no more and now, only Blizzard-Boy existed.

Chapter 4

Aqua-Gal was going everywhere in the academy to show me around. From the classrooms to the training rooms, everything was exquisite. I couldn't believe the number of rooms in the building. I was even taken aback when Aqua-Gal told me there were many basement floors as well. The training rooms I could use were all the same. There was a small arena on the left that had different targets and settings that could be adjusted based on the power or element. The right side was a meditative area to relax and calm the mind. After the main tour, Aqua-Gal took me to the dining area.

"This is where you go for your meals," she said. "It's all free and there are many different options to choose from."

"So, I don't ever have to cook again?" I said jokingly.

"I wouldn't go that far," she said. She leaned in and whispered, "I would avoid Taco Tuesday for your sake."

I laughed as she guided me to a table with three other supers. She waved to them, and they all waved back. I nervously waved and followed Aqua-Gal.

"Guys, this is Blizzard-Boy," Aqua-Gal said. "Blizzard-Boy, these are my friends Flama, Psycha, and Elect-Man."

"Hi," I said to them.

"Hey Blizzard-Boy," they said back.

I studied each of them carefully. Flama had deep red brunette hair and crystal blue eyes. She had small studs in her ears and her hair fell to her shoulders. Psycha had brown hair that was a little shorter and had hazel eyes that seemed to pierce my soul. She was a little taller than Flama, but not as tall as Elect-Man. He had jet black hair that was super short and had yellow eyes. I assumed they were contacts, but I felt rude asking.

"Where are you from?" Psycha asked me.

I turned to her and said, "I live on the outskirts of Motrac. It's right across the bridge where the chemical plant used to be."

Flama's eyes widened. "You're that boy that Aqua-Gal saved, aren't you??" she asked.

"Flama!" Aqua-Gal said.

"What? It's a legitimate question," she said.

I nodded. "Yeah, it was a strange night," I said. "I'm not even sure how all of this is happening."

Elect-Man looked at me. "You're not a normal super, are you?" he asked me.

I looked down nervously. "To be honest, I don't even know how I got my powers," I said. "I know it sounds lame and even weird, but it happened while I was in the hospital."

"I can believe it," Psycha said. "There's nothing strange about it. Other supers may see it that way, but the four of us are pretty unique when it comes to our powers and how we got them anyway."

I nodded and proceeded to tell them about my story. From the moment I found out about my parents to when I got my powers, they all seemed intrigued by my story. The more I told the story, the more I believed what was happening. It was becoming easier for me to adjust talking to the four of them.

"Wow, that is interesting," Flama said.

"I don't think anyone else has a story close to that," Psycha said. "However, my story is relatable in the family sense. When I was about 6, I learned about my powers from my mom who was a superhero. My dad was a normal human, so I had about a 50 percent chance of having superpowers. When I discovered my powers, my mom trained me and worked with me. My dad was nervous about this because being a superhero has so many risks to it. He wanted to keep it a secret, but my mom wanted me to develop my powers."

"One day when I was 8, I came home to my dad crying. He told me that my mom had been killed while on a recon mission. I couldn't stop crying with him. The day I told him I wanted to continue her legacy, he wanted nothing

38

to do with me. He couldn't bear to deal with the thought of losing two people he loved. I saw it as a chance to live through my mom's legacy and hold up the family name."

Flama nodded. "I had my powers as a little girl," she said. "Both of my parents were superheroes that went on dangerous missions. My dad got hurt bad on one mission to Lava-Top Volcano and that's when he settled down to recon missions. My mom quickly became a teacher at one of the other academies. They've been working with me since a kid training me to be a strong superhero."

"For me, I led a normal life," Elect-Man said. "My parents knew about my superpowers and helped me keep it a secret until I decided I was ready to be a superhero. Then I came here, and my parents support me. My story is much more boring than the others."

I chuckled and looked at Aqua-Gal. "What about you?" I asked her.

Aqua-Gal was taken aback. "Me?" she said nervously.

"Yeah," I said. "What's your backstory?"

Aqua-Gal looked down. "I don't think we need to worry about that right now," she said very quickly.

I immediately changed the subject, realizing I hit on a touchy topic. "So, have any of you been on exciting missions?" I asked.

Everyone shook their heads. "We're still young in the superhero sense," Flama said. "They usually reserve missions for supers that are advanced in their powers or that reach a certain age. We usually get set up with training simulations."

I nodded and heard a bell ringing. "That's the cafeteria bell," Aqua-Gal said. "It lets us know when classrooms are opening up for us to attend."

Flama and Psycha both stood up. "That means it's time for us to head to class," Psycha said. "The two of us have to work on team powers today and it's already complicated enough using my own powers."

"Hey!" Flama said. "Just because you can't understand my fire trajectory doesn't mean that I'm bad at this!"

The two of them continued to bicker as they walked off. I couldn't help but chuckle as Elect-Man stood up as well. He gathered his things and headed off to class as well. The cafeteria slowly emptied out and Aqua-Gal and I were left as one of the last few in the room.

"Do you have a class?" I asked her.

She shook her head. "I didn't want to say it in front of everyone because they would be jealous, but I actually got set up on a recon mission that doesn't involve patrolling the town," she said to me. "It's nothing too major but it is a change of pace."

"That's awesome!" I said. "When do you get back?"

40

"It should only take about two days," she said. "I can't say any more than that, but I'll fill you in on the details when I get back."

"Sounds good," I said. "Good luck out there!"

"Thanks," Aqua-Gal said. She stood up and walked out of the cafeteria. I decided to look in the training rooms to see what I was up against. I got up and walked out of the cafeteria. There were plenty of supers throughout the hallways talking as they waited for classes to begin. I had one more day before I would be in there. I walked to the elevator and pressed the button to go down a level to the training rooms. As I pushed the button, my hand froze to the button. I pulled as hard as I could to break out, but it was solid. I started punching the ice until my hand was free. The doors opened and some supers stared at me as I was shaking ice off my hand. My face grew red, and I stepped off the elevator to head to the training room.

I found the only training room that was unlocked at the end of the hallway: B45. I went in and turned on the lights. It was very spacious and smelled as though it had just been cleaned. I shut the door behind me and looked at the terminal. I turned it on and was greeted with a large menu with training options. I scrolled through until I found the new super registration and I pressed that. After a series of questions detailing my information, I was able to access all the options. I had no idea what some of the options meant so I started with a simple target practice. I pressed the start button and a series of stationary targets appeared.

I stepped in front of the terminal and aimed my had toward the first target. Nothing happened. I tried to focus and will the ice out of my hand, but it wouldn't go. I then thrusted my arm thinking that would launch some ice. Instead, ice dripped out of the palm of my hand onto the ground in front of me. I put my arm down and sighed. I picked up the ice clump and chucked it at the target. I hit the target and it went down. I decided that I wasn't ready for this yet and turned off the targets. I then walked over to the meditation space and sat down.

I closed my eyes and tried to focus. Instead, my mind kept wandering to the times before I was a superhero. All the times in school to all the times I spent in the park with my family. My head was spinning and my mind racing. I couldn't keep focus and found myself dripping ice again. I sighed and knew that it was going to be a long road ahead of me. I got up and made my way to the door of the training room. I turned out the lights and stepped outside. I made sure that the door closed behind me, and I then turned back toward the elevators. As I turned, I accidentally bumped into someone.

"I'm so sorry!" I said quickly. I reached my hand down to help them up.

"You should watch where you are going," the person said. He pushed my hand away and got up. "You never know when someone is going to be around you."

I pulled my hand back and just looked at him. "I didn't mean to run into you," I said.

The person brushed the front of their shirt off. "It's done with now," he said coldly.

"Umm… I'm Blizzard-Boy," I said hesitantly.

"Aero-Man," he said to me. "I take it you're new around here?"

I nodded. "I was just admitted today," I said. "I just got my powers the other day."

Aero-Man looked at me sharply. "You just got your powers the other day?" he said carefully. "That seems highly unlikely. All the supers here have their powers from an early age."

"I mean, it's true," I said. "I couldn't believe it either, but I woke up in the middle of the night with ice covering the bed."

Aero-Man studied me carefully. He walked around me and looked me over. I stood tense, unsure of what was going on. He mumbled some things to himself before coming back over to face me. I couldn't get a read on what he was thinking, but I was getting uneasy.

"Tell me… do you know exactly what happened to cause this?" he asked me.

I then began telling Aero-Man about the night the Zalcia plant exploded. From the moment it occurred to when I woke up in the frozen bed, Aero-Man was focused hard on my words. He was very intrigued and wouldn't stop staring me down. Once I finished, he nodded his head and turned around. He then began walking away.

"Where are you going?" I asked him.

Aero-Man continued to walk away. "I have some things I need to research," he said.

"Well nice to meet you," I said casually.

Aero-Man didn't say anything as he disappeared onto the elevator. I couldn't make any judgements about him, but I decided not to worry about it. I shook my head and walked to the elevators again. I got on and pushed the button to go back to the lobby. Everything was beginning to overwhelm me, and I needed to go home and take it all in. I was excited about being a superhero, but my life was being flipped upside down extremely fast. The elevator pinged and opened to the lobby. I got off and made my way to the front doors. I turned around one more time and looked at everything. I knew this was my future, but it was still difficult to accept.

I turned back to the doors and made my way home. I knew I had a long day ahead of me tomorrow.

Chapter 5

I woke up earlier than my alarm clock and groaned. I always hated waking up sooner than it and this was no exception. I climbed out of bed knowing that it was only six in the morning, and I could have slept another hour before getting up. I slipped and fell as I put my feet down and realized that ice had poured out of my hands onto the floor during the night. I grabbed my hip and carefully got back up. Shaking my head, I shuffled over to the door and made my way into the hallway.

I went downstairs and grabbed some salt for the sidewalk and carried a cup of it back to the bedroom. I tossed the salt on the ice and went back downstairs. I made my way to the kitchen and started digging in the cabinets. I found some cereal and grabbed a bowl. After making my breakfast, I sat down at the table in silence. This was the first time being back in the house since that night and it was different. I ate my cereal while staring at the wall and thinking back to the memories of my parents. I knew I had to get to a point where I could move on, but it was still so fresh in my mind. It had only been about four days, but I wanted to be able to move forward from it so badly. I took a deep breath and grabbed my dirty dishes to take to the sink.

I made my way to the bathroom to grab a shower before I made my way to STAT. I climbed in and turned the water on. In an instant, the water hitting my skin began to slowly freeze and I realized that my powers were forcing ice out of my body as the water made contact. I made my shower as quick as humanly possible to avoid being trapped inside an ice block and then I got out. While drying off, I had to pick off some ice pellets that had stuck to me and then I made my way back to the bedroom.

I grabbed some clothes out of my dresser and got dressed. It was weird still being in normal street clothes while attending STAT, but there was no word on any type of dress code. I grabbed my shoes and slipped them on and then made my way back downstairs. I grabbed the notebooks, pencils, and binders that I had laid on the table and placed them into a backpack. I slung the bag over my shoulders and made my way to the front door. I stopped as I grabbed the doorknob and looked back. The empty house behind me brought a tear to my eye, which then quickly froze and made me hold back my emotions. I picked off the tear and turned back to the door. I opened it and made my way to STAT for my first official day at the academy.

Passing through all the streets of Motrac was bittersweet. I watched as vendors called out to people to buy their products, children screaming and laughing as they chased each other, and cars making their way to work. Every step I took got lighter and lighter as I got closer and closer to STAT. As I rounded the final turns, I could see STAT appearing in the distance. My pace went from a slow walk to a brisk jog. When I finally got to the front doors, I could see Aqua-Gal sitting on a bench outside of the academy reading. I slowed my pace and walked over to her.

"What are you reading?" I asked her.

Aqua-Gal looked up and smiled. "Hey Blizzard-Boy," she said. "I'm just reading through some materials of the areas that I'll be scouting out."

"I thought you were going to be on a mission today," I said.

"That's what I'm reading through," she said. "I'm supposed to be leaving around eight to start my mission so I'm preparing myself for the environment to stay low."

I nodded. "Are you excited?" I asked her.

"I'm more nervous than anything," she said. "I've never been on a recon mission, so I don't know what to expect."

"I think you'll do fine," I said to her reassuringly.

Aqua-Gal smiled. "You're too kind," she said. "What about you?"

"I'm pretty nervous," I said. "I don't know what to expect and I'm afraid my powers will quickly become a hindrance."

"You'll be fine," she said to me. "The classes you're going into are designed for newer superheroes and many students will be in a similar position as you. Not necessarily in terms of how they got their powers, but more of how little control they have."

I nodded and looked back at the academy. It was still early, but I wanted to be able to go in and train early. "Are the training rooms open?" I asked Aqua-Gal.

She shook her head. "The only rooms that are open are the ones for supers that are finished with the beginning program," she said. "Since I'm going on a mission, they won't let me into a room so I can't get you into one. They want me to be as rested and prepared as I can be."

"Oh ok," I said.

"You can sit next to me," she said. "I don't bite… or at least that's what people have told me."

I chuckled and sat down next to her. We conversed for a while as the sun crept over the mountain tops. The rays of light slowly illuminated the academy, and all its details could be seen. Aqua-Gal and I talked and laughed for a few more minutes before students began arriving at the building. She then stood up and stretched.

"I should get ready to head in and meet up with my coordinator," she said.

"Coordinator?" I asked her.

"There are different coordinators for several types of missions that are brought in to do briefings and help prepare us for what's ahead," she said to me. "There are two coordinators responsible for the recon missions."

I nodded. "Then I'll probably meet up with Fraxion and figure out where I'm going," I said.

"That sounds like a good idea," she said to me. "I wish you the best of luck and I'll see you in two days!"

"Thanks, and be safe on your mission," I told Aqua-Gal.

"That won't be a problem," she said.

She waved to me as she started into the building, and I waved back. I grabbed my backpack and put it over my shoulders again. I got up and made my way through the front doors. I then walked up to the receptionist desk.

"Hey Sammy," I said.

Sammy turned to me and smiled. "Hey Robert!" She said.

"It's Blizzard-Boy now," I said. "I'm officially a part of the academy."

"Congratulations Blizzard-Boy!" she said. "I take it you want to meet up with the Superleader?"

I nodded. "Is he here yet?" I asked her.

"Yes, he actually just went to his office," Sammy said. "You can head on back there and I'll let him know you are coming."

"Ok, thank you so much," I said.

I made my way past the reception desk and walked back to Fraxion's office. I turned the corner and walked up to the door. I knocked on it and waited. The door opened and Fraxion was standing there.

"Come on in Blizzard-Boy!" Fraxion's voice boomed.

I stepped into his office and closed the door behind me. I walked over to his desk and sat down in the chair across from it. He sat down in his chair and rustled through some papers. He then looked at me and smiled.

"Today's the big day," he said to me. "You start your classes and your time as a superhero officially begins!"

I nodded. "I can't say I'm not nervous though," I said honestly.

"Don't worry son," he said to me. "There are plenty of new supers who are in your shoes. You're not the only one who is nervous about this. It's a new beginning and new beginnings can be scary. However, if you grab the bull by the horns and you really soak in what will be taught to you, then you'll do fine."

He handed me a couple papers and got up from his desk. I looked over the papers and they each were about the different classes I would be taking. The first class was on controlling my powers. It was slated to start around nine and lasted about two hours. The other class dealt with the roles that supers play in the world. This class also showed that it would last two hours and started

51

immediately following my first class. There was no official end date for when I was finished with the classes for good.

"These are the two courses you must complete to graduate from the basic program," Fraxion said. "I'm sure you've noticed that there is no end date for the courses. This is because each person has a different time frame for which the courses are to be completed. As such, you could complete these courses in one day or one year. It's all about the pace at which you refine your powers to be controlled and how long it takes for you to understand the superhero roles. These are important cogs to your time as a superhero and a firm foundation for many of your future missions. Heed these lessons well."

I nodded. "I'm assuming the rest of my day is for studying and training?" I asked.

"The rest of the day is for however you see fit," Fraxion said. "Some supers choose to go home and do deep meditation or relaxation and that's fine. Others choose to train and enhance their skills beyond what is taught in the classes. It's a matter of what you feel will work best for you. Just remember that missions are not an option for you until you graduate from the basic program."

"Understood," I said.

"Good," Fraxion said. "Now, head on out to your class. I don't want you to be late on the first day. Good luck and stay strong son!"

I got up and made my way out of Fraxion's office. I started down the hallway and began to look for classroom AR-7765. The third paper that Fraxion had given me was a detailed map of the academy. I followed the map down the corridors and eventually reached the correct hallway. My classroom was at the very end of the hall on the right. I made my way down there and sat on the ground outside the room. It was just turning to eight, so I still had time before the class began. I closed my eyes and tried to slow my breathing and heart rate. I figured this would help prepare me for the classes and the day ahead.

I began to doze off when I heard footsteps coming down the hallway. I quickly opened my eyes and saw someone coming toward me. They waved to me, and I waved back. I saw a key in their hand, so I figured it was probably the professor.

"Good morning," he said to me.

"Good morning," I said back. I got up and reached my hand out. "I'm Blizzard-Boy."

The professor walked up to me and shook my hand. "Nice to meet you," he said. "I'm Professor Cralic, but you can just call me Professor C."

"Nice to meet you Professor C," I said.

"I take it this is your first day?" he asked me.

I nodded. "I got my powers the other day," I said.

Professor C grew intrigued. "You just got your powers you say?" he asked me. "I'm not sure how that's possible."

I shrugged my shoulders. "You and me both," I said. "I wish I knew the answers to that one."

"How interesting," he said to me. "Nevertheless, my goal is to help you learn to control your powers to be able to be an effective superhero. I'll open the classroom so you can find a seat. I'm going to run to the lounge and get some coffee before class starts."

Professor C took his key and unlocked the classroom. He opened the door and we both stepped in. He placed his bag on his desk and then left the room. I picked a seat close to the front of the desk and sat down. I placed my backpack under my chair and grabbed a spiral and pencil out of the bag. I looked around the room and took in all the surroundings.

There was one large chalkboard at the front of the room with a large moveable white board off to the side. The professor's desk was standard and sat up front and center. There were about ten student desks in the room and plenty of posters along the walls. The classroom was not enormous, but it was large enough to have a sizeable class. As I took in the surroundings, more students began to show up. The class only had ten students in it, so there weren't a lot of us in the room. Professor C came back into the room and closed the door behind him.

"Welcome to class," he said. "My name is Professor Cralic, but you can all call me Professor C."

"Hi Professor C," the class said.

"This class is on controlling your superpowers," he said. "Some of you in the class already have a grasp on part of your powers, while others have just finished growing into the full extent of your powers. As many of you know, you get your powers at an incredibly young age. Many times, they lie dormant until a certain age where they slowly show their form. At this point, you begin to experiment with your powers. As time passes, you reach the age of allowance for STAT, and you can enroll here to further control your powers. This is where you all stand today."

"My goal is to be able to give you knowledge about your powers and help you achieve the meditative state necessary for reaching total control of your powers. As of right now, your powers act on a whim. They will activate under their own conditions or if stress levels reach a certain point. By achieving a deep meditative state, you can lock your powers into a state of pure control where you and only you can activate them. Until that state is achieved, your powers will continue to work on their own."

As Professor C continued to talk, I could feel my hands getting cold. I glanced down and saw small patches of ice beginning to form on my hands. I quickly crossed my arms and tried to hide it. It didn't work out as Professor C noticed a piece of ice fall to the ground.

"Blizzard-Boy is everything alright?" he asked me.

My face got red, and I laid my hands on the desk to show the ice forming in my hand. Professor C walked up and examined it. "This is a perfect example of what I had mentioned," he said. "Blizzard-Boy was sitting here listening to my lecture and his powers activated on their own and created ice in his hands. This is nothing to be ashamed of as all beginning supers experience this in some way or another."

Professor C then went back to the front of the class and began detailing the methods of meditation. I broke the ice off my hands and grabbed my pencil to start jotting notes down. I could see small slivers of ice dripping down from my hand onto the pencil and I would stop every few seconds to break it off. After Professor C finished all the methods, he then had us find a section of the room and work into a meditative state.

I chose an area close to the window so that I could use nature to help reach a meditative state. I stared out into the trees and sky and observed all the birds and animals. The wind had a slight breeze that caused the leaves to gently sway. I closed my eyes and focused on that serenity. I let the calm wash over me and I worked to find peace inside me. I could feel the meditative state slowly coming over me. As I continued to find peace, it was broken by the thoughts of my family. I tried to suppress it, but the more I worked to suppress it, the less focus I had on my meditative state. Eventually, the bell sounded in the room and class was over. Instead of reaching a meditative state, I found myself sitting in a ring of ice. I sighed and got up. As I started toward the door, Professor C stopped me.

"After your next class, come back and see me," he said. "I want to work on something with you," he said.

I nodded and walked out of the door. Frustration started washing over me and I couldn't get rid of it. I made my way to my next class and continued to think about what I could do to break the burdens.

Chapter 6

I finished my second class and made my way back to Professor C's classroom. I still hadn't gotten over my frustration. I couldn't understand why every time I tried to meditate that the same thoughts kept creeping up on me. I knocked on the classroom door and walked in. Professor C was sitting in the back of the room in a meditative state. I quietly closed the door and waited.

"Come over this way," Professor C said to me.

I walked over and sat down across from him. He opened his eyes and looked at me. "Blizzard-Boy, do you know what my powers are?" he asked me.

"No, I don't," I said.

Professor C stood up and walked up to his desk. He reached into his bag and pulled out a thick notebook. He came back over and sat down. "I have two very unique powers," he said. "One power is the ability to read and interpret negative energy. It sounds like a very useless power, but it is extremely effective in therapy and superhero training. This is the main reason I have dedicated my time and energy into teaching. My second power is to be able to release positive energy into the air that can be absorbed by others."

"That is unique," I said.

"Many people think I'm a hippie because of this, but it is far from the truth," he said. "The energy that I release actually calms the mind and spirit and can form a protective cloak from villains who might be able to sense negative energy. It is also extremely useful in meditative states."

I nodded. "What does this have to do with me?" I asked.

"Earlier today, I could feel a very strong negative energy coming from within the room," he said. "There was plenty of negative energy, but the energy I felt coming from you was so strong that I couldn't even focus my positive energy outward. I instead focused in on your energy and interpreted it."

I hung my head. "So, you know what I was thinking then," I said.

Professor C shook his head. "That's where many of my students get confused," he said. "My ability to interpret negative energy does not give me the ability to read minds. I can only interpret the energy in terms of what kind of negativity you are experiencing. I only know that this energy was a burning traumatic experience. Beyond that, I do not know."

"It's a complicated story," I said.

Professor C put his hand on my shoulder. "I can tell this experience is still recent," he said. "It is too much for you to suppress in one shot. That is what is holding you back. There are multiple energies stemming from this event. You are trying to suppress the entire event to achieve your meditative state. As such, you are unable to maintain the focus on meditation necessary to achieve deep meditation."

"What should I do?" I asked him. "Every time it comes up, I can't control my emotions."

"Start small," he said. "What is the thing that angers you most or causes the most emotion?"

I started thinking carefully. "I think the fact that I couldn't stop it," I finally said.

Professor C nodded. "That is the focal point of most traumatic experiences," he said. "*Focus* on suppressing that area and you will find that your focus can reset again. Do this routinely and eventually the energy will dissipate, and your focus will become clearer."

"Won't fully suppressing it cause me to forget everything?" I asked.

"No," he said. "As you suppress the thoughts, you will be slowly coming to terms with what has happened. You will begin the acceptance phase of the healing as you come to terms with the event. You will only be suppressing the negative thoughts and energy associated with it rather than the event itself. It will no longer become a distraction and rather a memory that you can look back on more fondly than you are able to at this current time."

I nodded and closed my eyes. I worked to focus myself on the deep meditative state. I could feel myself becoming peaceful. Just like earlier, my family began to come back to my thoughts. This time, I focused on what was angering me and I could see the hatred in myself for not being able to stop it from happening. *No,* I said to myself, *there was nothing I could do. This was an accident that I couldn't have prevented. I know my family still cares about me and knows that I was not the one responsible.* I continued to push this thought through and I could slowly feel the energy being suppressed. The meditative state pushed away, and I found myself opening my eyes.

"That's it," Professor C said. "You've begun the process. It will take time—and a lot of it—for you to fully erase the negative energy, but you are on the right track. Continue this on your own and you will find that controlling your powers will become much easier."

"Thank you, Professor C," I said.

Professor C smiled. "I only told you what you needed to do," he said. "You are the one conquering your demons."

I smiled and got up. "I'll see you tomorrow," I said to him.

Professor C nodded. "Bright and early."

I walked out of the room and felt calmer. I knew I had a lot of work ahead of me, so I decided to head to a training room. I figured I could meditate further and try to really set myself up for success. I made my way to the elevators for the training room and saw Aero-Man standing there.

"Hey Aero-Man," I said to him.

61

He looked up at me and scoffed. "You're impossible," he said.

"Excuse me?" I said.

"The way you gained your powers. The events leading to it. The genetic background. You should be impossible," he said. "There's no logical evidence to show how you could have gained your powers."

"I don't know what else to tell you," I said. "I'm in as much shock as you are."

Aero-Man stared at me. "Are you positive that your family does not have any possible superhero links in it?" he asked me.

"If there is, I was never told," I said.

Aero-Man looked me over again. "You know that the Zalcia should have killed you," he said. "There are absolutely no chemicals within the compound that would give any normal human superpowers."

I shrugged my shoulders. "I guess I'm not a normal human then," I said.

Aero-Man looked at his notes. "There is a missing link to all of this, and I won't stop until I've found it," he said.

Aero-Man turned and walked away from me. I focused my attention back on the elevators as one was opening for me. I got on and made my way down to the training rooms. As the door opened, I saw Psycha standing outside of a training room. I walked up to her.

"What are you up to?" I asked her.

Psycha turned to me. "I'm watching one of the newbies train," she said. "I always like to study superhero training tactics so that I can implement some useful ones to my training regimen."

"Why not watch more experienced supers?" I asked.

"Many of the veteran heroes are stuck in their ways," she said. "They find one way of training and stick to it. I like to be diverse for any situation. New superheroes tend to be more experimental in their training and it gives me new ideas."

"I never thought of that," I said.

"Most veteran supers don't either," she said.

I nodded. "I'm going to go meditate in one of the training rooms for a while," I said to her.

She nodded to me. "That's a good idea," she said. "Especially since it's your first day."

"I'll see you later!" I said to her.

I made my way down the hallway to the training room I used last time and went in. I skipped past the training area and went straight for the meditative area. I sat down and began my focus. No matter what it took, I was going to find a way to control my powers.

Chapter 7

The first two days at STAT were relatively the same. I spent a lot of time meditating to control my powers. Each day I felt progressively closer to achieving the deep meditation I needed. I had graduated from my second class easily, especially since I had done so much research on the superhero lifestyle as a kid. All I needed to do was learn how to control my powers. I walked into class for my third day and Professor C greeted me.

"You are making strong improvements," he said to me.

"I took your advice and I've been doing a lot of meditating," I said. "It's really helped me in more ways than one."

"The positive energy you are emitting is much stronger than before," he said. "I would imagine you are not far off from achieving total control."

I smiled and sat down in my seat. I heard some of the other students mumbling behind me. I listened closely to what they were saying.

"Yeah, some super got caught during their recon mission," one of them said.

"I heard that she set off a trap and that's what got her," another one said.

"I think it was Aqua-Gal," a third one said.

I immediately spun around. "Did you say Aqua-Gal??" I asked quickly.

The first student nodded. "She was on some recon mission and a villain caught her," he said.

"Class, we are ready to begin," Professor C said.

I turned around, but my level of concern was now high. I was trying to process how Aqua-Gal got caught on a recon mission. Was it more dangerous than she made it out to be? Was she just careless? I needed to know more information.

"Blizzard-Boy, please focus," Professor C said.

My face got red as I realized that he could catch the energy I was putting out. "Sorry Professor C," I said apologetically.

Professor C nodded and began his lecture again. I tried not to think about what was going on with Aqua-Gal, but it was hard to not be worried. When we sat down for the meditation, I decided I needed to try to focus harder than normal on controlling my powers so that I could graduate out of the basic program. I got into my meditative state and the negative energy slowly poured in. I took a deep breath and forced myself to not even put any focus on the thoughts. Because I didn't try to suppress it, it started pushing harder. I continued to ignore it, but I could feel my focus slowly slip. I controlled my breathing and my heart rate and used my pulse as a balance point.

The negative energy was pushing hard on me. Emotions were about to start welling up. Just then, I could feel a different energy surround me and I knew it was Professor C. I immediately calmed myself and focused on that energy instead. As I did, I could feel all that negative energy dissipate and my focus returned to my meditative state. Now, I could feel myself slipping into a deep trance and I knew I was close. I entered a deep meditative state and could feel the calm around me.

I then focused on my powers. I focused on what I wanted out of my powers and the absolute control of them. I could feel the energy of my powers becoming more contained. With each passing moment, my powers became more confined and accurate. After a few minutes, I could tell that my powers were under my control. I slowly worked myself out of the meditative state and slowly opened my eyes. I looked at Professor C and smiled.

"What is it Blizzard-Boy?" he asked me.

I stood up. "I think I have control of my powers," I said.

Professor C looked at me. "Follow me then," he said.

I followed him out of the room and to the room across the hall. In this room, there were several targets lined up. Professor C stood to the side as I took my stance in the middle of the room.

"You have ten targets," he said. "You are allowed only ten shots. Make them count."

I heard a buzzer, and I immediately knew what to do. I lifted my hand, pointed it at the first target, and shot ice at it. Direct hit. I could feel a smile coming on my face. I pointed at target two and did the same thing. Another hit.

"Keep going!" Professor C said.

I quickened my pace and threw my other hand up to alternate shots. I was ecstatic. Each shot resulted in a hit on the target. The sound of the target hitting the ground was satisfying and when I finished, all ten targets were down.

"Blizzard-Boy," Professor C said. "You were allotted ten shots."

I immediately froze. In my excitement, I hadn't been paying attention to the number of shots I took. I knew what was coming and I slowly turned to Professor C. "How many did I go over?" I said nervously.

"That's the thing," he said. "You didn't go over. In fact, you only used nine shots."

I stood there shocked and then I remembered. On my ninth shot, I had decided to create a beam of ice that spanned the length of two targets. I was afraid now that I had broken the rules and was going to be forced to retake the test tomorrow. However, Professor C stuck out his hand and I shook it.

"Congratulations," he said. "You successfully passed!"

I smiled. "I can't believe it!" I said.

"You've officially graduated from the basic program," Professor C said. He scribbled something on a piece of paper. "Take this to the Superleader.

He will officially graduate you and you will have full access to all of STAT. You will also have new opportunities available to you that you didn't have before."

"Thank you so much!" I said happily. As I took the paper, Professor C looked me in the eyes.

"Do not forget your training," he said. "Just because you have controlled your powers does not mean that energies cannot cloud your judgment or ability to use your powers. Your powers are under your control, and it is up to you to enhance your abilities."

I nodded. "I won't forget," I said.

I turned and made my way back down the hallway. I had controlled my powers just like that and was now ready to take on the world! I turned the corner and made my way down to Fraxion's office. I approached the door and knocked. There was no answer. I waited a bit and then tried again. Still no answer. I turned back down the hallway and walked up to the reception desk.

"Hey Sammy, is Fraxion here?" I asked her.

Sammy looked up and smiled. "He should be almost finished a meeting," she said. "He's down in conference room FC-266 if you want to meet him over there."

"Thanks, Sammy," I said.

I turned and started down another hallway. I hadn't been down this way before because it was usually reserved for faculty and meetings. I carefully followed my map and turned a few corners. I eventually found the room and heard voices coming out of it. I sat next to the door and tried to listen.

"We have no idea what we are up against," One person said.

"Another recon mission should be in order," another one said. "Preferably one with a little more *experience* this time."

"Recon missions are no good now," a third voice boomed. I could tell it was Fraxion. "We now have a captive superhero that needs extraction so the time for recon is over. We must act and act now before something happens."

"The problem is we don't have a strong core of superheroes that could potentially take on this kind of challenge," the first person said. "Bring us some ideas tonight and we will contemplate the ramifications of such actions."

I heard some rustling and mumbling and then some footsteps approaching the door. I got up quickly and stood further off to the side. The door opened and I watched as four supers stepped out and walked the other direction. I didn't recognize any of them. Then, Fraxion stepped out and saw me.

"Blizzard-Boy?" he asked. "What are you doing here?"

"Sammy sent me this way to find you," I said. "She said you were finishing up a meeting."

"I keep telling her not to send students down this way," he said. Fraxion looked at me. "What do you need from me son?"

I handed him the paper. "Professor C told me to give this to you," I said.

Fraxion looked over the paper and smiled. "Well son, it looks like you are already done the basic program!" he said. "That was rather quick! Please, follow me back to my office and we will proceed from there."

I nodded and followed him back to the office. The whole way there I kept thinking about what I heard. I knew they were talking about Aqua-Gal, and I wanted to say something about it, but I didn't know how it would be perceived. We reached his office and Fraxion unlocked the door for us to enter. I sat in the chair again and he sat down in his.

"Let's start with this," he said. He took the paper and began typing some stuff on the computer. After a couple minutes, I heard the printer in the back of the room come to life. Fraxion got up and grabbed something off it. He handed it to me.

"This is your keycard," he said. "As a graduate of the basic program, you will need this keycard to access the other facilities of STAT. Do not lose it as it contains valuable information. If you do lose it, report it immediately so it can be deactivated and a new one issued."

I nodded. "Thank you, sir," I said.

"You are now also eligible for missions," he said. "For now, you would be best suited for recon missions, but all options are available under the proper circumstances."

"I want to rescue Aqua-Gal," I immediately blurted. I then quickly covered my mouth as Fraxion stared at me.

"You overheard the meeting I assume?" he said.

I hung my head. "I did," I said. "I also overheard a lot of rumors throughout the day."

Fraxion leaned back in his chair. "Let me explain the extent of the situation to you," he said. "Aqua-Gal was sent on a small recon mission in the outer edge of the Fastik Forest. This is where it was rumored that a villain base was located. As such, this forest resides only 25 miles outside our radius and sparked a lot of concern from superheroes. This mission was designed to locate and map the location of the base."

"Unfortunately, the area around the base was well fortified with traps and one such trap managed to alert villains in the base to Aqua-Gal's presence. Within minutes, she was captured and her GPS signal lost. We know which villain controls the base as well as its location, but that is all we know. As of now, we are trying to determine our best course of action before this gets out of hand."

"Who is the villain?" I asked.

"The villain has been determined to be Magnowing," Fraxion said.

"I've heard that name before," I said. "He's been around for a while, hasn't he?"

Fraxion nodded. "He's never really been a threat until recently," he said. "He usually has small plans that we are able to stop, but this is a serious problem. As long as he has a superhero hostage, he holds all the cards."

"I'll do it," I said.

Fraxion shook his head. "You just graduated from the basic program," he said. "I can't risk that."

I looked down and then back up. "Then let Psycha, Flama, and Elect-Man join me," I said. "They've been working hard to go on a mission like this and I know they care about Aqua-Gal like I do."

Fraxion took a deep breath. "There are so many risks associated with this and you haven't even had time to train," he said.

"Let me present my case tonight," I said. "Same for the others. We'll train together today and have some strategies prepared for this."

Fraxion stood up and looked out the window. "You have four hours to train, prepare, and strategize," he said. "You will present your strategy to the board at five and they will determine if it is worth the risk. Your comrades must also be one hundred percent committed to taking on this mission before I will allow you to speak in front of the board."

72

I nodded. "I won't let you down."

Fraxion turned around. "You must understand something, Blizzard-Boy," he said. "This is not a comic book or a game. Superhero lives are at stake and one wrong move can result in lost lives. I'm not trying to scare you; I'm trying to put perspective on this mission. Do not do anything rash that would put yourself or any other superheroes in danger."

"I won't, sir," I said.

Fraxion nodded. "Four hours," he said. "I want you to bring your strategies to me first before we go over."

I nodded and walked out the door. I took a deep breath and realized what I had just committed to, but I didn't care. I wanted to make sure that Aqua-Gal came back safe.

Chapter 8

"Hey Blizzard-Boy," Psycha said to me.

I sat down at the cafeteria table with Psycha, Flama, and Elect-Man and looked down. Flama studied me and leaned in. "Are you ok?" she asked.

"Did you guys hear about Aqua-Gal?" I asked. Everyone shook their head. "She was captured on a recon mission."

Everyone was silent. "Why didn't anyone say anything to us?" Flama asked.

"Honestly, no one was saying anything," I said. "I found out from rumors and overhearing the Superleader talk about it."

Elect-Man shook his head. "How do they plan on getting her back?" he asked.

I looked away and was immediately met with stares. "Blizzard-Boy, what's going on?" Psycha demanded.

I turned to them. "I talked to the Superleader and stated that I wanted to rescue her," I said.

"That's madness!" Flama said. "You just learned to control your powers!"

"I know," I said. "I also volunteered you guys to come along too."

"WHAT???" Psycha shouted. "How could you do that??"

"None of us have experience like that!" Flama yelled.

"Dude, we'd get destroyed!" Elect-Man yelled.

"I thought the four of us together would be able to handle it," I said. "I figured you guys have a lot of experience with your powers and would want to save Aqua-Gal."

"We ALL want to save Aqua-Gal," Psycha said. "None of us feel comfortable going after a high-powered villain."

"Who is the villain anyway?" Elect-Man asked.

"It's Magnowing," I said.

Flama shook her head. "There's no way I'm doing this," she said. "It's way too risky!"

"We may be her only hope!" I said.

Psycha got up. "Sorry, Blizzard-Boy," she said. "I'm not signing up for this."

Flama stood up as well. "I can't either," she said.

Elect-Man followed suit. "Sorry, dude," he said. "We'll be served on a silver platter against Magnowing."

The three of them left and I was left alone at the table. I didn't know what to do. I was desperate to do something to save Aqua-Gal, but I knew that I would struggle by myself. Plus, if the three of them weren't on board with the plan, then Fraxion wouldn't let the plan commence. I decided I was going to go to the training rooms and try to plan and strategize on my own. I would even create some plans that would include everyone in case something happened.

I got up and made my way out of the cafeteria. I turned to the elevators for the training rooms and started toward them. Everyone was laughing and making their way to their classes, but I was focused on the task at hand. I had less than four hours to plan and strategize and I needed to make the most of it. I got to the elevators and got on. Instead of going down to the training rooms I had been using, I went up to the new ones that I was eligible to use. I had to swipe my keycard for the elevator to take me there. Once it registered, the elevator began its ascension.

I started thinking about different possibilities. I didn't know much about the terrain in the Fastik Forest, so I was strategizing blind. I did know that Magnowing's base was rumored to be near the center of the forest, but that was about it. If Aqua-Gal had managed to be captured in the forest by a trap, then I knew Magnowing would have the place booby trapped like crazy. I needed to be stealthy and alert to avoid detection. *At least my powers are controlled,* I thought to myself. *Now I don't have to worry about leaving an ice trail.*

The doors of the elevator opened and that's when something hit me. I immediately ran into a training room and closed the door. These rooms were much larger with a different terminal set-up. There was also a scoreboard and timer on the wall, presumably for tournament practice or timing missions. The terminal allowed for the changing of terrain to prepare for any situation. I found a table in the corner and sat down. I grabbed some paper and a pen and began writing out some ideas.

I had turned the timer on in the training room to count down from two hours. I wanted to focus all my attention on the strategy and not have to worry about watching the clock. I drew many diagrams and wrote several plans, scribbling them out as time passed. The ones that I thought had the best opportunity I kept circled and the rest found their way into the trash can. I looked up at the clock and it read fifty-two minutes. I decided that now was the time to test out the four plans I had remaining to determine the best option.

I got up and changed the terrain to resemble the Fastik Forest. Trees and bushes began appearing and I watched as animals spawned in. Everything was digital in the sense that if it got destroyed, it was not realistic. Slamming into a tree or stubbing your toe was still very real so I knew I needed to practice as though it was real. I set the terminal to place several different types of traps ranging from camouflage to heat sensitive. Once everything was set, I stepped into the forest. It wasn't the entire forest, but it was a large enough portion that I could get the gist of what I would be up against.

I started walking slowly, watching each and every step for signed of abnormalities for traps. Nothing was jumping out immediately, but I knew it wouldn't be long. Once I got partway into the forest, I decided to try my first tactic. I focused my energy and powers and felt my core temperature slowly drop. My body heat was not leaving me; I had it carefully focused into my core. Instead, I had focused my ice powers to create a chilled shell over my body heat. By doing this, my plan was to prevent any heat sensitive traps from activating.

My first test came shortly after the preparation. I peered around a tree and saw a small disk on the ground. It had a tiny light illuminating from it. I immediately recognized the device as a heat sensitive mine. It had the ability to trigger if it detected body heat within 50 feet from it. One of the biggest things about this trap was its unique ability to cloak itself with the light if it sensed body heat drawing near. Because the light was still white, I knew it hadn't sensed me yet. I was less than 50 feet away from it.

I slowly walked toward it, taking care not to make any sudden movements to trigger other traps. My plan was to disable the trap to make it useful to me later. The light continued to stay white. I continued toward it slowly, all the while focusing my energy on the shell to make sure my heat was being contained. Unfortunately, that required a lot of focus, and I could tell I was slowly losing it. Just then, I saw the light on the mine slowly shift to mimic the surroundings. I knew that my cover was blown, and I needed to run. I turned and started, but that set off the mine. The explosion threw me forward and I clipped a tree on the way to the ground. The terminal shut off the terrain and I was left lying in the middle of the floor in pain.

I groaned as I slowly got up. I brushed some dirt off and clutched my shoulder. It wasn't out of place, but it hurt like crazy. I walked back over to the table and crossed that plan off my list. I looked at the timer. 22 minutes. I didn't have time to try anything else. I needed to try training against an AI before I went to Fraxion so that I had a little battle experience. I walked back over to the terminal and set up the battle. I made sure to give my opponent lightning powers to try to mimic what I believed Magnowing would possess. Once it was set, I started the battle.

I stepped onto the field as the digitization of the opponent finalized. My opponent was named Lightno.1 in relation to the settings I had chosen. I dug my left foot into the ground and prepared myself. The buzzer went off and Lightno.1 charged toward me. I stood my ground and leapt in the air. I shot ice down at it creating a slippery patch, but it used its lightning to shatter the ice. I landed on the ground and immediately got slammed into by Lightno.1. It pinned me to the ground and jumped up. I watched as a charge of lightning came from its hand toward me. I rolled out of the way just in time, but not before another beam came down and struck me.

I screamed and laid there. I slowly got up and saw Lightno.1 land on the ground near me. I shook my head and charged toward it. Lightno.1 read my move and charged itself up. I could see the lightning coursing around its body, and I knew what was coming. I quickly turned to run past him and threw ice behind me to create a wall. The lightning blast hit the wall and shattered it but dissipated before it reached me. I turned and saw that Lightno.1 was no longer there. I began to shoot ice in different areas of the floor to make it slick. Just then, I saw it out of the corner of my eye launching a lightning blast at me. I turned and blasted a beam of ice at it. The ice was breaking just as quickly as it was reaching the lightning, but I wasn't giving up.

At the last moment, I jumped to an ice patch letting the lightning zip past me. Lightno.1 refocused his fire at me, and I took that opportunity to jump from ice patch to ice patch. The lightning was hitting each patch and reflecting in different directions. I then turned and spun in a circle while creating ice. It wrapped in a ball above me, and I captured the lightning within it. I then focused the ice toward Lightno.1 and the ice ball rolled toward it. It waited to jump until it was right there, but I took that moment to break the ice. The lightning inside charged out in every direction and several beams struck it. Lightno.1 hit the ground and I quickly shot ice blasts at it. The simulation stopped and I had won.

I looked back at the timer and saw I had less than ten minutes remaining. I sighed and gathered all my things. I walked out of the training room and made my way to the elevator. I pushed the button to head back down to the main floor. As the elevator went down, I started thinking about what I was up against.

I must get them to believe that I can handle it, I thought to myself. *Even though I am inexperienced, I know I have what it takes to save Aqua-Gal. I can't let her remain captured by Magnowing!*

The elevator doors opened, and I stepped out. I made my way back to the main lobby and headed toward Fraxion's office. I reached the door and hesitated. I knew what was about to come and I needed to make sure I was ready to plead my case. I slowly reached my hand up and knocked on the door. I waited for Fraxion to open the door, all the while I was sweating bullets. The door opened and Fraxion was standing there.

"Please, come in," he said.

I nodded and obeyed. I stepped in and Fraxion closed the door. I noticed there were four chairs in front of the desk and my heart sank. I knew this was not going to go well.

"I presume that the others are on their way?" he asked me.

"Well… about that…," I said hesitantly.

Fraxion stared at me hard. "Blizzard-Boy, you know the stipulations," he said. "I cannot let you do this mission on your own."

"Please just hear me out," I said. "I have some decent strategies."

Fraxion turned away and walked to his desk. "It is not the strategies that concern me," he said firmly. "My sole responsibility at this academy is to ensure the safety of all the students here. As such, I am obligated to make decisions on certain missions based on the capabilities of a student as well as their abilities. Unfortunately, you do not have any credentials to your name yet regarding missions or experience in the superhero realm. You have only been here a few days and have just gained your powers."

"I know I can do this," I said. "I have been training hard and strategizing."

Fraxion turned back to me. "Training simulations are not the same as actual villains," he said. "Training simulations have a set of guidelines they must follow, namely, to not kill anyone. Villains do not have guidelines to follow. If they want to kill you, they will do so."

"I know this isn't a game," I said. "I care about Aqua-Gal, and I want to rescue her. Every moment spent not working to rescue her is another moment closer that Magnowing could decide to kill her."

"I know the risks associated with this," Fraxion said. "However, I do not want to risk the lives of two superheroes because of inexperience."

I looked at the ground. "Fraxion," I started. "I know I won't fail."

"That's right, because we're going with you," someone said behind me.

82

I turned around and saw Psycha, Flama, and Elect-Man standing at the door. I began to smile as they stepped into the room.

"Superleader, sir," Flama started, "We want to go on this mission."

Fraxion looked over at all of us. "You are all one hundred percent in agreement?" he asked carefully.

"Yes," Flama said.

"Absolutely," Psycha said.

"Sure," Elect-Man said. Flama elbowed him and Elect-Man grabbed his side. "I mean yes, sir."

I looked back at Fraxion. "Does this mean we have a chance to present our plan?" I asked him.

Fraxion took a deep breath. "You may present your plan," he said. "After that, I will decide if it is worth bringing up to the board. You may all contribute as you see fit."

We all nodded and sat down in our chairs. It was time to detail the plan.

Chapter 9

Fraxion looked over the papers one last time and then looked at us. "This plan doesn't seem too bad," he said. "There are a few risk spots, but overall, it should work."

"Does this mean we can present to the board?" I asked him.

Fraxion nodded. "Understand though that they have the final say," he said. "They are higher ranking than I am and have the ability to overrule the decision."

"When do we present to the board?" Flama asked.

"They will be here in about two hours," Fraxion said. "You have until then to train, relax, or do whatever you need to do."

Psycha stood up. "We should go and get something to eat really quick and discuss the plan again," she said. "It's important to close any holes that might linger in this mission."

"I second that," Elect-Man said. "I'm starving."

"You and me both," Flama said. They all got up and started heading to the door.

"You coming Blizzard-Boy?" Psycha asked me.

"Yeah, I'll be there in a minute," I said.

They all nodded and left the room. I looked back at Fraxion. "Thank you," I said to him.

Fraxion looked at me. "You don't need to thank me son," he said. "You presented a plan to me that makes sense and if it meets the board's approval, you will have the chance to rescue Aqua-Gal. That's what being a superhero is about. You must be willing to take initiative and push yourself to the limit. Had you presented a broken plan, I would not be allowing you to speak to the board."

I nodded. "You still didn't have to say yes to us," I said. "I know I'm new in all of this."

Fraxion put his hands together. "Son, you have a fire that I haven't seen in a long time," he said. "I've been the Superleader for almost thirty years and most students don't show the drive that you showed me."

"I just care about Aqua-Gal," I said.

"You care about everyone," Fraxion said. "I can tell in your personality. Now, go meet up with the others. I'm sure they're waiting for you."

I nodded and got up. As I started toward the door, Fraxion stopped me one more time.

"Don't ever let your friends go," he said. "They will be your foundation throughout all of this."

"I won't," I said to him.

I walked out of the office and shut the door behind me. I sighed and wiped the sweat off my forehead. The stress from that was more than I had anticipated, but I knew I wanted to have a chance to save Aqua-Gal. I walked down the hallway back to the lobby and then started toward the cafeteria. I walked in and saw Psycha, Flama, and Elect-Man all sitting at a table with food. They waved me over and showed me the tray of food they got for me. I smiled and walked over to them.

"What made you guys change your mind?" I asked them.

Flama pointed at Psycha. "She's the one who convinced us," Flama said.

Psycha shrugged her shoulders. "I knew how much of an impact Aqua-Gal had on you and all of us," she said. "I don't think this academy will be the same if we don't rescue her."

I sat down and started chowing down on my food. I looked up at everyone and saw they were all laughing. I looked down and saw food all over my shirt. I quickly grabbed a napkin and started cleaning it up.

"You know Blizzard-Boy, even though we just met I really feel like you have been a part of the group forever," Flama said.

"You fit in, that's for sure," Elect-Man said.

"I appreciate you guys being so friendly and helpful to me," I said.

"You're part of us now," Psycha said. "If Aqua-Gal thinks highly of you as a friend, then you are friends to us too."

I nodded. "I just hope she's ok right now," I said.

"I'm sure she is handling herself," Elect-Man said. "She's a feisty one."

I laughed and we continued to eat. We started going over the strategies again and what we would need to do. Ideas were tossed around and discussed. Slowly, a final detailed plan began to come to fruition, and I knew it would work. Once we finished, I got up and stretched.

"I think we should use the last hour of our time to train," I said. "We should work on some of our fighting tactics in case we would get into some trouble."

"Sounds good to me," Flama said.

We all got up and dumped our trash in the trash can. We then made our way out of the cafeteria to the training room elevators. We kept talking and strategizing all the way to the elevators when I noticed Aero-Man standing near them again.

"Hey Aero-Man," I said.

He looked up briefly and then looked back down at his book. "Don't you have things you need to take care of?" He said snidely.

Flama scoffed. "What's his problem?" she said.

"Don't worry about him," I said. I looked at Aero-Man. "We're going up to train for a mission."

Aero-Man snickered. "You just controlled your powers and you think you'll be successful on a mission?" he asked. He closed his book and looked at me. "Just because you are unique in how you got your powers doesn't mean you are all powerful. Don't let it go to your head."

Aero-Man turned and walked off. Psycha shook her head. "I don't even know anything about him, but I already don't like him," she said.

I shrugged my shoulders. "He seems rough, but I'm sure he has a lot going on," I said.

Elect-Man pondered for a moment. "Come to think of it, I don't even remember seeing him here before," he said. "He must be new."

"He never said," I said.

"Huh," Elect-Man said. "I guess it doesn't matter now. Let's get to the training room before we run out of time."

I nodded and pushed the button for the elevator. We filed in and Psycha pushed the button. I swiped my keycard and the elevator doors closed. It slowly crept up to the floor we needed and opened. We all stepped out and found the first available training room. Flama closed the door behind us, and Elect-Man walked up to the training module.

"We need to make sure that we are accurate," he said. "If our shots are not calculated to do the most amount of damage, it will eat away precious time. I say we focus on some accuracy challenges so that we can make the most of any battles we may find ourselves in."

"Sounds like a plan," I said.

"I'll go first," Flama said.

Flama stepped onto the field and Elect-Man pushed some buttons. Ten moving targets appeared in various speeds. Elect-Man then changed the terrain to the forest to simulate the environment.

"You have ten targets and ten shots," Elect-Man said. "If you use more than that, you'll have to start over."

Flama nodded and raced toward one of the trees. She ducked down and waited. Out of nowhere, a target sliced past her and she took that moment to launch a fireball at it. She led the target and it landed right on the bullseye. She turned around to see two targets moving from tree to tree. She launched another fireball after memorizing the pattern and it connected. Two targets down. Flama continued moving around and studying the targets, following that up with a well calculated shot. After her tenth shot, the final target came down.

"Not bad," Elect-Man said. "You had a perfect accuracy, but you took a lot of time."

"You only said I had to be accurate," Flama said. "You said nothing about speed."

Elect-Man shrugged his shoulders. "It's however you want to do it," he said.

Flama rolled her eyes and sat down. Psycha got up and made her way to the field. Elect-Man reset the targets and Psycha began her turn. She positioned herself in the middle of the forest. All ten targets were moving around her. She quickly glanced at each one before closing her eyes. Suddenly, the air around her began to shift and leaves started circling her. She opened her eyes and moved her arms. As she did, the leaves formed into small balls. She created ten of them and compressed them, causing the leaves to shift into pure energy. She then turned and quickly threw all ten of the balls. Each one went toward their own target and homed in on them. Like a fireworks display, the sky lit up with the energy as well as the debris from the targets.

"Ten for ten," Elect-Man said. "Great speed as well."

Psycha turned to him. "As long as I can have enough time to focus, I can perform moves like that all the time," she said.

Psycha came off the field and Elect-Man motioned for me. I got up and took my position on the field. I hadn't done anything like this since I had controlled my powers, but I knew what I needed to do. The new targets appeared, and I ran to a nearby tree. I quickly scaled it, causing a series of gasps from everyone else. Once I reached the top, I saw all ten targets popping in and out of the forest. I crouched and launched myself in the air. As I did, I started to spin and shoot ice. Crystals began to form around me, creating an updraft. I continued to spin, and more crystals formed. I then stopped and clapped my hands together. The ice crystals clashed together and exploded into five ice balls. As I began falling, the ice balls headed toward the nearest targets. When I hit the ground, I heard the explosion of all ten targets and I looked at Elect-Man.

"How did you... You hit all ten with only five shots?" He said in shock.

Flama stood up. "Blizzard-Boy, that was amazing!" she said.

My face grew red. "I mean, I watched a lot of superhero movies growing up," I said. "Plus, I did a lot of research as a kid."

"That move is impressive, but also highly dangerous," Psycha said. "If you do that in the Fastik Forest, Magnowing will see you over the treetops for sure. If you use a move like that, save it for if you come face-to-face with him."

I nodded. "I have other ideas of moves and tactics that I can use," I said. "I just wanted to try that to see if it would work."

Elect-Man motioned for me to the terminal. I walked over and he showed me what I needed to press for his turn at the training. He walked onto the field and I turned on the targets. Elect-Man disappeared into the forest and we all waited. Suddenly, a blast of lightning shot out and struck two targets at

91

once. More blasts came out and within seconds, the ten targets were demolished. Elect-Man had only fired seven shots before downing all the targets. He stepped out of the forest and looked at everyone.

"Not as impressive as Blizzard-Boy, but I have my set of moves too," he said.

"It seems like we should be fine," Flama said. "We just need to make sure we are stealthy and avoid as many battles as possible."

"Magnowing will have plenty of traps once we get deep enough into the forest," I said. "We just have to watch out for each other."

Elect-Man nodded. "I think it's time we headed down to the conference room and presented our plan to the board," he said.

I nodded in agreement. "We have to answer every question to the best of our knowledge," I said. "The board will immediately reject us if we can't prove that this plan will work or that we are capable of it."

Everyone agreed and we made our way out of the training room. We walked in silence to the elevator as each of us were focused on the objective at hand. No one wanted to mess this up. Aqua-Gal's life was at stake, and we all knew how dangerous this was going to be. The doors opened and we filed in. We pushed the button to head back down and Flama sighed.

"This is going to be our first mission if we get approved," she said.

"It's also going to be the most dangerous one available," Psycha added.

"We'll be fine as long as we stick together," I said. "I know Aqua-Gal would have the utmost faith in us."

The doors opened and we stepped back out. We made our way down the hallway and back to the lobby. I told everyone to wait while I walked up to the desk. Sammy saw me coming and smiled.

"What can I do for you, Blizzard-Boy?" she asked.

"I need to know where the board meeting with Fraxion is taking place," I said.

"Of course," she said. She turned back to her computer and started typing. After a few seconds, she turned back to me. "The meeting is going to be in conference room FC-301. It's the farthest room down the third hallway in the conference sector."

"Thanks Sammy," I said. I turned back to the others and motioned for them to follow me. We made our way down the corridor and turned down the third hallway. We made our way to the end and saw the room. The door was open and we could hear voices inside. We looked at each other, took a deep breath, and stepped inside.

"Good evening, students," Fraxion said to us. "We are just about to begin the meeting."

Chapter 10

Flama, Psycha, Elect-Man, and I each took a seat next to Fraxion. There were three other superheroes in the room as members of the board.

"I would like to introduce you each to our esteemed members of the board," Fraxion said. "They are also members of the High Council of Heroes. This is Thantianos, Prosistric, and Loudorn. I have already told them about each of you."

Thantianos had dark hair and appeared to be short. He had piercing grey eyes and a deep voice that filled the room. Prosistric had brunette hair and she was very tall. Her eyes were a deep ocean blue and her voice was soothing as she spoke. Loudorn had no hair and was blind. His voice was soft spoken at times, but he could project very easily.

"I appreciate you four taking time to present your plan to the board," Fraxion said to us. "They are very eager to hear what you have to say."

"Please, enlighten us on your plans to rescue Aqua-Gal," Thantianos said. "If your plan makes sense and has a low risk factor, then we will consider allowing the four of you to go on this mission."

I nodded and stood up. I walked up to the front of the room and faced everyone. I looked over the room and took a deep breath.

"As many of you know, Aqua-Gal was captured by Magnowing the other day," I started. "She was on a recon mission that went wrong and resulted in her capture. The four of us have teamed up to create a strategy and plan that should effectively allow us to infiltrate Magnowing's base and rescue Aqua-Gal without causing any harm to a super. Each of us will contribute our unique abilities and skills to achieve this goal."

"Our first objective is to get to the Fastik Forest without our presence being detected. Knowing that Magnowing has the forest littered with traps gives us an idea that Aqua-Gal may have been detected before she even got to the forest. With this in mind, we will not use a traditional method to reach the forest. After examining certain things about the forest, we have discovered that there is a large clearing right before the forest. That clearing could have been where Aqua-Gal was detected. Rather than going in through the main clearing, we will start by going in from the side via the mountain range from the west."

"The mountain range will provide the necessary cover we need in order to sneak into the Fastik Forest without initial detection. Once inside, we will use our stealth and abilities to maneuver through any traps that might be set in the forest. By focusing our powers, we can potentially hide our body heat from being detected by any heat sensors in the forest. There is the possibility of some mines as well as cameras in the forest. By having a small radius around each of us, it makes it difficult—if not impossible—for us to be detected all at once. This means if anyone trips a trap, we are in the perfect set-up to trigger an ambush of the villains who may appear."

"Once we have located the base, Elect-Man will proceed to find an outside port that he can data mine the map of the base. Once that has been completed, Flama and Psycha will team up to find the weak point in the building and use a controlled flame to melt a hole in the wall with Psycha bending it down. We can then proceed in the base, locate Aqua-Gal, and escape without any further detection."

There was silence after I finished speaking. I could see each of the members of the board deep in thought. Fraxion was leaning back in his chair patiently waiting and watching. It was Loudorn who was the first to speak up.

"Won't going through the mountain range prove to be more treacherous than approaching from the front?" he asked.

I shook my head and realized what I had done. "No, it won't," I said. "If we approach from the front, it will jeopardize our mission before we even begin. The mountain range is not too bad if we come in from the right spot of the mountain. There is a small path that will allow us to scale most of it."

"What about once you get in the base?" Prosistric asked. "You never specified the plan inside the base other than to find Aqua-Gal."

"Honestly, we don't have a full plan yet because we don't know the layout of the base," I said.

"Maybe we should start with that before we pursue action," Thantianos said. "If we can get the map of the base, we will be able to plan further."

Fraxion stood up. "We can't do that," he said. "That would require one superhero getting the data without being detected."

"Yet here we are discussing four YOUNG superheroes infiltrating a well-known villain's base," Loudorn said.

"You're missing the point," Flama spoke up. "If someone goes in initially to get the map and come back, Magnowing will know he's been compromised and could adjust accordingly."

"We don't know that for sure," Prosistric said. "The only thing we do know is how dangerous this mission is going to be."

"That's just it," I said. "It doesn't matter how we look at this scenario. It is going to be dangerous regardless of how we attack it. We can't afford any more recon missions or possible short-term decisions. We must make a big move now before Magnowing realizes that we are slowly making a move and he either comes after us or kills Aqua-Gal. I know we are young, but we have been training and planning this for a reason. We care about Aqua-Gal, and she is a huge asset to STAT."

Thantianos nodded. "We appreciate your concern for Aqua-Gal, but our biggest problem we see is the inexperience and the youth of the four of you," he said.

Fraxion leaned toward them. "I believe in these students," he said. "It sounds hard to believe, but the bond they share between each other as well as their determination provides more experience than many of our older supers. We have to give them a chance. For the sake of Aqua-Gal and for STAT."

Prosistric leaned back in her chair. "This is not an easy decision; you must remember that" she said. "The High Council does not take lightly to major tasks like this. However, the circumstances have changed, and it does seem as though the four of you are more mature than your years would show. However, that does not mean mistakes will not be made."

"Mistakes will be made," I said. "I won't deny that. That's why our plan is designed the way it is. We will have each other's backs and be able to learn from each other. If we don't make the mistakes, we can't learn from them to grow."

"I appreciate your honesty in all of this," Loudorn said. "I believe that this may be our only chance at rescuing Aqua-Gal. As a member of the board, I vote yes to this mission."

I began to slowly smile as Thantianos began to speak. "I have reservations about this mission," he said. "I just can't see risking a total of five superheroes as opposed to one or two. I have to say no to the matter."

I could feel my gut twisting inside me. The fate of the mission came down to Prosistric. She continued to lean in her chair as she pondered. I wanted to say something and make a plea, but I knew that it could potentially make the situation worse. Prosistric sighed and leaned forward.

"I hesitate to make this decision knowing the impact it could have on the future," she said. "My head tells me to feel one way. However, my heart leads me another. I must go with my heart. I will say yes to the mission."

We all looked at each other and smiled. "Thank you, everyone," I said. "We won't let you down."

Thantianos looked at me and it felt like he was staring into my soul. "Do not fail," he said firmly. "Prove me wrong. If you succeed at this mission, the four of you will be eligible for any mission available. Understood?"

"Yes," we all said.

Thantianos turned to Fraxion. "If this mission fails, you will be the one to answer for it," he said.

"They won't fail," Fraxion said.

Thantianos nodded and looked to Prosistric and Loudorn. "I think it's time we went back to the council," he said.

They each nodded and got up. They left the conference room and I sighed.

"Your mission begins at dawn," Fraxion said. "We must tackle this early."

I nodded. "We'll be ready," I said. "We'll strategize a little more and then get some rest."

"We'll be ready," Flama said.

Psycha nodded. "We'll get Aqua-Gal back," she said.

"You can count on us!" Elect-Man said.

Fraxion nodded and left the room. I looked at everyone and smiled. "Thanks for doing this, guys," I said.

"You really don't need to thank us," Flama said. "Let's just get to the training room and do some meditation before we have to get some rest."

We all got up and headed out of the room. We made our way back to the elevators and went back to the training rooms. Each of us took our own rooms to meditate. I closed my door behind me and walked to the meditation area. I sat down and slowed my breathing. I decided to channel my power to help me focus. The cool ice coursed within my body and I could feel my heart calming down. I began to meditate and focus on the mission at hand.

This is my chance to prove I can be a superhero, I thought to myself. *Aqua-Gal is relying on us to be successful. I don't want to let her down. I don't want to let the others down. I don't want to let myself down.*

My focus was so deep that I didn't notice when someone had entered the room. I jolted when I felt a tap on the shoulder. I looked up and saw Psycha standing there.

"Mind if I sit with you?" she asked.

"Not at all," I said. I patted the ground next to me.

Psycha sat down next to me and slowed her breathing. I did the same and we both went into a meditative state. After several minutes of this, we both sighed and looked at each other.

"I always find it easier and soothing to meditate with someone else," Psycha said.

I nodded. "I'm still getting used to it," I said.

"I can imagine it would be hard," Psycha said. "With the situation you were thrust into, it can be difficult to channel the energies in the correct way."

"It's gotten easier," I said. "I guess I just needed time."

Psycha put her hand on my shoulder. "Don't let the negative thoughts cloud you," she said. "It's easy to get caught up in that. Continue to meditate and focus like you are. We will all be here for you through it as well."

I smiled. "Thanks, Psycha," I said.

She smiled back and stood up. "I'm going to head home and get some rest," she said. "Do you need someone to wait with you?"

I shook my head. "I should be fine," I said. "Motrac isn't the busiest place in the world."

Psycha chuckled and walked out the door. I took a deep breath and got up. I did a few stretches and then made my way out of the room. I closed it behind me and headed toward the elevators. I pushed the button and the door opened. Aero-Man was standing in there. I stepped in and pushed the button down. The doors closed and it started down. Just then, Aero-Man pushed the emergency stop button and the elevator jerked to a stop.

"What are you doing?" I questioned him.

Aero-Man looked at me. He grabbed me by the collar and threw me into the wall. He then pinned me there and stared straight into my eyes with his piercing green gaze. I cringed and waited for a punch to be thrown.

"I don't know who you think you are, but you need to cut the hero crap out," he said coldly.

I gave him a puzzled look. "What are you talking about?" I said confused.

"You are not a normal superhero," he said. "You are not going to be the one who is going to always save the day. Just because your precious friend is kidnapped does not mean that suddenly you are an all-powerful superhero. I've been training for years for those kinds of missions and I'm NOT going to have you get in the way of that!"

"Aero-Man, calm down," I said. "There are plenty of missions for everyone."

Aero-Man balked at me. "Don't tell me to calm down," he said. "I can wipe you out in an instant!"

I started to look around for a way out, but Aero-Man had me locked in place. I tried to struggle forward, but he pushed me harder into the wall.

"Listen to me, and listen well," he said. "This mission will be your first and last mission. I will not have you trying to upstage my opportunities at greatness! I have been passed over too many times to let a pipsqueak like you ruin my chance! Understand?"

I nodded in hopes that he would let go. He continued to stare at me before letting go. He backed up and started the elevator again. I stood there in stunned silence as he watched me. The elevator pinged and the doors began to open. He held the door close button.

"If you even think about telling anyone about this, I will end you," he said. "Don't test me on that either."

He let go of the button and the doors opened. He stepped off and disappeared before I could do anything. I got off the elevator and stood there. *What just happened?* I thought to myself. *He just attacked me out of nowhere! I have to tell someone!* I started to head toward the lobby to head to Fraxion's office, but I stopped. I didn't know what Aero-Man was capable of and I certainly didn't want to find out. I decided to just head home and keep my guard up.

I had a long day ahead of me anyway.

Chapter 11

I woke up to the sound of my alarm going off at five in the morning. I carefully reached over and shut it off. I stretched and felt a twinge in my neck. It was sore from when Aero-Man has thrown me into the wall. I still had no idea why Aero-Man had done that in the first place. I didn't have time to think about it though. I got out of bed and quickly got ready for the day. I grabbed a shower and got dressed. I then grabbed a quick breakfast and made my way out of the house.

I strolled through Motrac one more time before the big mission. I began to reminisce about my life before I became a superhero. All the times I went to the markets with my family, all the times I hung out with friends, all of it came rushing back. I felt a tear come on as I knew that this was officially the end of that lifestyle. Once I embarked on this mission, I would no longer be able to return to the life I once knew. I had to rescue Aqua-Gal though.

I reached STAT and saw Psycha, Flama, and Elect-Man standing outside talking. I walked up to them and waved. They waved back and the twinge in my neck struck. I quickly put my arm down and met up with them.

"You ok, Blizzard-Boy?" Flama asked.

I nodded. "I think I just slept wrong," I lied.

"At least you got sleep," Elect-Man said. "I couldn't get to sleep until three in the morning."

Psycha laughed. "That's what happens when you can't stop playing your games," she said.

I laughed and saw Fraxion walking up to us. We all turned as he got closer. "Good morning everyone," he said.

"Good morning," we all said to him.

"Are you all prepared for this mission?" he asked.

I nodded. "We're ready to save Aqua-Gal," I said.

Fraxion smiled. "I have faith in you guys," he said. He then pointed to a car nearby. "I'll drive us to the edge of the Fastik mountain range on the west side of the Fastik Forest. Once you scale the mountain, I will head back to the academy. Once you have rescued Aqua-Gal and have left the base, press this button and I will immediately return to the rendezvous point."

Fraxion handed me a small button. It had a small case over it so it couldn't be accidentally pressed. I placed it in my pocket.

"I think we have everything that we need," Flama said. Everyone nodded.

"Let me go into my office to get the keys and then we'll head off," he said.

Fraxion disappeared into the school. I turned to the others. "I hope Magnowing hasn't done anything to her," I said.

"If he did, he'll have to deal with all four of us," Flama said.

I nodded and looked over at the car. This plan was elaborate, but it still made me nervous. I had never been in this type of scenario before, and I didn't know what to expect. Fraxion came back out and we all headed to the car. Elect-Man sat in the front, and I sat on the right side in the back with Flama and Psycha. Fraxion turned the key in the ignition and the car roared to life. He backed it up and then turned onto the road. He looked both ways and then started forward.

I looked out the window and watched the scenery go by. Trees and houses were passing by. I closed my eyes and tried to meditate one last time. I controlled my breathing and slowed my heart rate. I focused on the mission and Aqua-Gal and made sure that I was dialed in. We hit a small bump and it knocked me out of my meditative state. I looked over at Flama and Psycha who were talking to each other. They were laughing and carrying on. I turned back to the window and continued to watch things go by.

Aqua-Gal, don't worry, I thought to myself. *We're on our way to rescue you.*

To be continued…